T0095494

TRINA'S CHRISTMAS GIFT

OPAL WATKINS

ISBN: 978-1-4669-0523-8 (sc)
ISBN: 978-1-4669-0522-1 (e)

Trafford rev. 11/30/2011

 www.trafford.com

North America & International
toll-free: 1 888 232 4444 (USA & Canada)
phone: 250 383 6864 ♦ fax: 812 355 4082

Chapter One

The air, biting and cold, penetrated Trina's worn coat and caused her to shiver. The hurried along the broken sidewalk feeling glad that school had let out for the holiday vacation. Snow covered the ground. Trina bowed against the wind and held tightly to her books. Since her parents were involved in an automobile accident early last spring life had been hard for Trina. Her father lost his life in the accident, and her mother remained an invalid. With no relatives from either side, Trina of necessity became the one in charge of the family at the tender age of twelve.

Now Trina's greatest concern was to find a way to give her brothers a nice Christmas. With precious little money even for the necessities Christmas gifts were out of the question unless Trina could think of a way to earn some money, or a miracle was headed in their direction.

Trina watched the children at play as she walked along. She knew that it would be a wonderful vacation for them. She looked down at her worn brown loafers and realized how cold her feet were. She curled her stiff fingers tighter around her books and broke into a run.

"How's your Mama, Trina?" Mrs. Howell called as Tina passed by her gate.

"About the same, Mrs. Howell," Trina answered.

"Last day of school, huh?" she asked.

"Yes, until January second," said Trina.

"Guess your Mama will be glad to have you home all day. I am proud of you and the boys. You still managing alright?" Mrs. Howell questioned.

"Sometimes it isn't easy, Mrs. Howell. But we are doing fine," she said.

"Well, it's nice you have a few days off. You come visit me when you can," Mrs. Howell said.

Trina smiled, and said. "I have to get home now, goodbye,"

"Bye, bye, Dear," Mrs. Howell answered. She turned and walked toward her house with her two cats Pansy and Calico purring and rubbing around her ankles.

Trina ran the two blocks to the lane that led to the house where she lived with her mother and two brothers. She sighed as she looked at the snow covered lane broken only by three sets of footprints made by her and the boys this morning as they left for school. No returning prints showed, so she knew that she was the first to return.

"I must try to shovel a path tomorrow," Trina muttered as she stepped into the snow and waded to the porch. The snow reached her ankles and her feet felt frozen. She opened the door and narrowed her eyes as the brightness of the snow contrasted the darkened room.

"Trina, is, that you?" a voice called.

"Yes, Mama." She walked into the bedroom and over to the bed where the frail, dark haired woman gave her a weak smile. Trina smiled back and gave her mother a kiss. She tidied the covers and moved around the room picking up tissues and straightening articles on the bedside table.

Her actions came automatically from long days and nights of practices,

"How do you feel, Mama?" she asked.

"About the same, dear. Is Danny and Joel home yet?" Her mother asked.

"No Mama, we got out early today because of the holiday vacation. I hurried home. I suppose the boys will be along at the usual time. Do you want to sit up now?" Trina talked gently to her mother as though the rolls were reversed and she were the mother soothing her child.

Tenderly she turned back the covers, placed her arms under her mother's and both working together, she soon rested in her wheelchair. Trina covered her with a worn blanket.

"What's for dinner?" The boys entered noisily, tracking snow into the living room.

"I am starting it right now," Trina answered.

"I'm starved," seven year old Danny proclaimed. "Hurry up, will you?"

"You boys take off your shoes and put them by the heater to dry." Trina delegated. "Joes, you set the table, and Danny you get a wash cloth and help Mama wash her face and hands."

Both boys dutifully obeyed after kissing their mother hello.

As Trina fixed dinner her thoughts went back to the days when her father was alive and mother was well. She remembered how happy they were in those days. They were certainly not wealthy, but she remembered frilly dresses and prized possessions, laughter and fun, as they did things an ordinary family does. She could see Daddy swing her high into the air when she ran to meet him in the evenings when he came home from work. Her mother smiling, waiting for his kiss.

Trina loved the evenings when her daddy played with her while mama did the dishes. Sometimes Daddy would help with the chores, then they would all go for a romp in the park.

Trina could see Mama as she ran joyously to retrieve a ball or Frisbee, her raven hair bouncing and shining. Her trim figure clad in jeans and top, Trina believed her to be the most beautiful woman in the world. How thrilled she felt when someone said, "You look just like your Mother."

Yes, Dan and Lorriane Bradley were a couple filled with happiness and peace as they enjoyed the present and looked forward to a glorious future.

Trina was three when Joel came along. She adored her baby brother and helped Mama care for him. She thought him to be the prettiest baby ever. He had dark hair like Mama's, and laughing blue eyes.

When Mama knew she was expecting another baby, she let Trina help her even more. How important and needed she felt as she looked after Joel and ran small errands for Mama.

They were all excited when the time came for Mama to go to the hospital. Trina and Joel stayed home with a neighbor lady to look after them.

Trina lay in her bed wide awake waiting for Daddy to come home. It was very late when she heard his car drive in. In a few minutes she heard him thanking Mrs. Gossage for staying with the children. Then the door closed and she knew her daddy would be coming down the hall to look in on her Joel.

She got up and opened the door.

"Trina, are you still awake, Baby? You shouldn't be up this late." He gathered her in his arms and carried her to the bed.

"How is Mama?" Trina asked. "Do we have our baby yet?"

Daddy laughed and said, "Yes. Another boy. Now you will be busier than ever helping Mama, huh?"

"Oh yes, I love to help. I am going to be a mama when I grow up just like my Mama, and have a husband just like you, Daddy." Trina said, as she hugged him tightly. Trina felt safe and good as Daddy's arms tightened around her. Then he tucked in the covers and kissed her goodnight.

"I love you Daddy." She said dreamily and immediately drifted off to sleep.

Baby Danny was six months old when one day Daddy came home early from work very excited.

"I am being transferred to Westville," he said, "It is a new plant opening up. They gave me a promotion and a raise. We are going to build a house with a big yard for the kids and plenty of privacy."

They packed that night and early the next morning set out to their new home. Upon their arrival in Westville, Daddy talked to a real estate agent *who* said he knew of a house that would be perfect for the family.

It needed some repair work, he said. But the price seemed fair so Daddy agreed to look the place over. Daddy slowed as they came near the end of the street.

"It's there at the end of the lane," Mr. Boggess the real estate agent said.

Daddy turned and rove up the lane to the house. It was marvelous. The tree lined lane broke away to reveal a wide yard, green and freshly mowed. Trees rose toward the skyline like silent sentinels. The house strategically placed in the grove stood looking peaceful and inviting, but in the obvious need of repair as Mr. Boggess had said.

The house boasted a large picture window in the living room, which Mama and Trina took to right away.

"Can't you just see it with white lacy curtains," Mama whispered, and Trina giggled with delight as she anticipated the fun the family would have fixing the place up.

They walked across a long wide porch with paint turned up, peeling and ugly. Mr. Boggess unlocked the door and led the way into the house. The living room was large and from the inside the large window gave a glorious view of the yard.

"I didn't realize the lane turned that much," Daddy said. He stood looking out the window. "The street is completely hidden from here."

"Yes," said Mr. Boggess. "The man who owns the place likes his privacy. If you want, you can clear away some of the shrubbery and trees easily."

"I like it this way," Daddy said. "Don't you, Hon?"

"Yes," replied Mama. "But the most important thing is the house. It sure needs a lot of work."

"Let me show you the rest of the house," Mr. Boggess said. There were two bedrooms upstairs. Trina and Joel especially liked them and stayed behind looking out the windows at the trees, and the huge backyard. There was a tall tree with low hanging limbs near the house, and Trina wondered what all you could see if you climbed it.

Trina and Joel sat looking out the window when Daddy slipped up and knelt behind them. He gathered them both in his arms.

"Well, what do you think of it, Trina and Joel?" he asked.

"I like it. I can climb the tree," Joel said bravely.

"Wait just yet, Joel," Daddy laughed. "But it will be fun when you are a little bigger. Trina, do you think you would like living here?"

"Yes, Daddy," Trina answered excitedly. "Please, may we buy it?"

"Yes, Mama and I have agreed. We are going to buy it. We believe it will be a wonderful home for our family." Daddy sounded enthusiastic.

The next few weeks were hectic as they moved in. They were busy from morning to night. Trina worked so hard that her legs ached at night when she lay in bed, but it was a marvelous feeling as the adventure of buying furnishings, cleaning, and deciding what goes here and what goes there culminated and they all stood at last admiring their handiwork.

The white lacy curtains on the picture window rustled gently in the breeze. The modest combination wood and plaid living room furniture looked homey and inviting.

"Not half bad for a low budget," Daddy said proudly.

The living room gave way to a sizable dining area. The door to the left led to the master bedroom which mama and daddy shared. Trina chose the upstairs bedroom nearest the big tree. True to her expectations when she climbed it she found that she could view the neighborhood. She and Daddy quickly named it the observation tree. The next seven years were remarkably happy. When Trina was eleven Daddy came home one day all excited. It reminded of the time when he had excitedly told them they were moving to Westville.

"I am going on a trip as representative for my company," Daddy said proudly. "Mama is going with me, but I am sorry, I cannot take you Kids."

Mrs. Howell from down the street came to stay with them until their parents returned. She proved to "b a kind, loving woman and they had fun as the children helped her do the chores. She suffered from arthritis and could not get around very well. They loved making cookies or popping corn and sitting around the living room while Mrs. Howell told stories.

Sometimes one of the tales would be especially spooky. Then Danny would press close to Trina and sit wide-eyed and captivated. They all became fond of each other as they waited for their parents return.

Trina will never forget the terrible Friday before Mama and Daddy were to be home on Sunday. A knock sounded on the door and when she opened it a tall policeman stood looking solemn and apprehensive.

"Is this the Daniel Bradley residence?" he asked.

"Yes," Trina replied hesitantly.

"May I ask who you are, little girl?" he queried.

"I am Trina Bradley. Dan and Lorriane Bradley's daughter." Trina said.

Mrs. Howell came to see what their visitor wanted. She paled when she saw the policeman.

"I am Mrs. Victoria Howell," she said, "I am sitting with the children while their folks are away on a trip. What do you want?"

"I am Officer O'Brian, Ma'am." He paused, looking strange and concerned. "I am awfully sorry to bring this kind of news, but there has been an accident." He said.

"Oh, my lord," Mrs. Howell gasped. She moved near Trina and placed an arm around her protectively. Trina tried to understand what the officer said, but it didn't make sense. He was telling them that Mama and Daddy were not coining home because they were involved in an accident.

Suddenly she panicked and yelled, "No, it's not true. My Daddy and Mama will be home on Sunday, Don't you see? They love us."

Officer O'Brian patiently allowed Trina to cry until the tears were spent and she sat wide-eyed and weak with Mrs. Howell's arm protectively around her. Then he explained how the accident happened;

Dan and Lorriane were on their way home and were only ten miles from the city when a fuel truck driver lost control of his vehicle and crossed the median striking the Bradley station wagon broadside. Both vehicles bounded over the edge of the roadway.

The station wagon, after spinning over and over came to rest upside down in a clump of bushes.

The gasoline in the fuel truck exploded on contact.

A couple passing by saw the explosion. The man stayed to offer assistance and sent his wife to call the police. By the time they arrived the man had located a woman between the roadway and the station wagon. She was unconscious. About fifty feet beyond where she lay he found a man who evidently was killed instantly and thrown out of the station wagon as it rolled down the embankment.

The truck burned furiously and he could not go near it, so he turned his attention to the woman. When the ambulance arrived the paramedics took over and rushed her to the hospital.

The police found her purse and identified her as Lorriane Bradley. Also in her purse was a man's wallet containing identification for Daniel Bradley. Trina thought of how her daddy often had mama carry his wallet in her purse when he was driving. The police sent the body to a mortuary. They searched the area for the truck driver after the fire died down enough to see that no one was in the truck.

The authorities were puzzled until they heard a moan only a few feet from where the deceased had been found. Officer O'Brian found the third victim. He cringed at the sight that greeted his eyes when he looked behind the bushes.

The man was severely burned. His face a scorched, bloody mass. His clothing charred.

"Over here," Officer O'Brian yelled.

"Good lord, it's the truck driver. He's in bad shape, get a stretcher over here," the Sargent yelled . . .

CHAPTER TWO

Mrs. Howell helped Trina make arrangements for the funeral,

"Is there kinfolk back where you come from you want to call, Child?" she asked.

"No, Ma'am. My Mama has no relatives that I know of. Her parents passed away and she was an only child," Trina explained,

"What about your Pa?" queried Mrs. Howell.

"My Daddy was an orphan. He had no one either. That is one reason why Daddy and Mama loved each other so much, Mrs. Howell. They both knew how it is not to have anyone. Now my Daddy is gone and Mama has no one again," Trina began to cry.

"Now Child, you hush," Mrs. Howell said kindly. "Your Ma has you and the boys. She will never have to be alone again,"

Both wiped tears as they made arrangements. The funeral was a simple one, Mrs. Howell managed to get a minister to conduct the service. He was a chubby, short man with a high pitch in his voice. When he shook hands with them, his hand was clammy and wet and Trina noticed how white it was. It seemed he was in a hurry, for he rushed away as soon as the service ended and they had not heard from him since.

The boy's still in shock from it all simply accepted Mrs. Howell and Trina's decisions. Even though Trina felt the service was lacking there seemed nothing to do but go home.

Mrs. Howell proved to be an anchor to the children as days passed and their mother remained in intensive care at the hospital. No visitors were allowed. Each time they called they received the same answer. Sorry, but Mrs. Bradley's condition remains critical. It was a time of strain and worry for Mrs. Howell and the children.

At last the day came when the nurse told them they could visit. Mama had been moved out of the intensive care unit to a room. They hurriedly made the trip to the hospital.

When they entered the room Trina could hardly believe the weak, pale woman on the "bed was her mother. She stood for a moment, uncertain of what she should do. Mama reached a hand toward her and said;

"Trina, I am so glad to see you. Come here."

Her color was very pale and she looked weak but managed a half smile as Trina walked toward her.

"Oh Mama. I have missed you so much. I love you," Trina exclaimed, as she threw her arms around her.

"Joel and Danny? How are my boys?" Mama asked.

"They're here, Mama," Trina said, and stepped aside to make room for her brothers.

Danny ran and embraced his Mama. Joel stood quietly. He was astonished at the way his mother looked.

Mama held Danny for a minute, then released him and held out her hand to Joel. Joel ran to her for a loving reunion. Soon the boys were chattering away with quiet acceptance of their mother's condition.

The nurse came to inform them that Doctor Morgan wanted to talk with them. Mrs. Howell and Trina left the boys to keep Mama company and walked down to the doctor's office. The door stood ajar and Mrs. Howell knocked softly to attract the doctor's attention.

"Come in," he said. He stood and shook hands with them.

"I am Doctor Morgan. Trina, your mother has been anxious to see you. I suppose you have been taking good care of your brothers haven't you?

"Yes," Trina answered shyly. "Mrs. Howell has been staying with us. When may Mama go home?"

"Well, that is something I wanted to talk to you about. You seem quite mature, Trina. Do you suppose you can understand if I explain your Mama's problem?"

"Of course she will, Doctor," Mrs. Howell said. "She is as sharp as a tack, and dependable. I will help her with whatever she needs. We stick together and make it just fine."

"That is wonderful, Mrs. Howe11," the doctor said. "It is a blessing the children had you to look after them. I am terribly sorry about the death of your father, Trina. Please, won't you both sit down?"

After they were seated Doctor Morgan began;

"Trina, do you understand what psychological means?"

"I think so," said Trina. "Doesn't it mean that your mind is sick?"

"In this case, that is right, Trina. Your mother was hurt in the accident but the physical problems are pretty well cleared up. I have talked at length with her about your father's death, but it hasn't become a reality in her mind yet. Do you understand what I am saying?"

"I think so. You mean that Mama does not believe that Daddy is dead." Trina answered.

"The problem is that Mrs. Bradley insists that her husband will return to his family and they will be happy as always. This sort of problem is not uncommon. Sometimes things come as such a shock the mind cannot comprehend the reality of what has taken place."

"What can we do, Doctor?" Trina asked.

"Well, I know it won't be easy, Trina. But I feel it would be better for your mother if she were at home with you children. The familiar surroundings may make her better able to cope with the fact that your father is not in the home anymore. She needs complete care. It will not be easy. I would be willing to release her if you feel you can care for her at home. I will make arrangements for a wheelchair to be delivered for you to use as long as you need it at no charge. So, what do you two think?" Doctor Morgan waited for their decision.

"I am willing to do what I can, Doctor," Mrs. Howe11 explained. "But I have arthritis and sometimes when I get inflammation in my joints I can hardly take care of myself. Trina and the boys are good at helping though. It's up to Trina. What do you think, Dear."

"Yes, I want to take Mama home. We will take very good care of her, Doctor Morgan. I promise," Trina said.

"Alright, let's try it, and we will talk more about it after we see how she accepts the home environment." Doctor Morgan agreed.

"Thank you, Doctor." Trina said, "I know Mama will be better soon when she is at home with her family."

Trina and Mrs. Howell started toward the door. Suddenly Trina turned and said;

"Doctor Morgan, I want to ask a favor of you."

"Yes Trina. What may I do for you?" Doctor Morgan answered.

"The man who hit Daddy and Mama. The truck driver. I would like to see him. May I?" Trina asked.

"Now Trina," Mrs. Howell began. "I told you this is to much for you to be concerned about."

"Why do you want to see him?" Doctor Morgan asked thoughtfully.

"I want to tell him that we don't blame him for the accident, and that we hope he will be well soon." Trina explained. "Please, Doctor. May I see him?"

"It may not be a bad idea at that," Doctor Morgan said. "But before I agree I must explain about what has happened to Mr. Smith. Since we did not find any identification we don't know who he is. Here at the hospital we needed a name for our records so we gave him the name David Smith. You see, Trina. Mr. Smith was badly burned and since the accident he has suffered a loss of memory. It is called amnesia. He remembers nothing prior to the accident."

"How are his burns, Doctor?" Mrs. Howell's curiosity began to surface.

"Still serious but much better. He has had three skin graft operations, and we think he will heal well except for some scars which are unavoidable. He should look quite presentable when the bandages come off. What we need now is something to bring him in contact with familiar things that were in his life before. There has been no response at all to the publicity concerning the accident. Since we have nothing of his past to work with, we will have to try to break through with getting him interested in something concerning the present." The doctor paused.

"Then may we talk to him?" Trina asked.

The doctor was impressed with Trina's concern and mature attitude.

"You are quite a young Lady, Trina. You know you have no real responsibility to Mr. Smith, but since you have such a loving heart it may be this is a beginning in helping him to cope with his life. I will allow you to see him once. Then we will go from there according to how he accepts your visit. You already have your job cut out for you. Agreed?"

"Agreed," Trina smiled.

Doctor Morgan led the way. When they reached the room he motioned for them to wait as he went forward,

"Dave, I have someone with me that I want you to meet," he said.

"Who is it?" The reply sounded weak and pathetic as though the man could care less about meeting anyone.

Doctor Morgan motioned for Trina and Mrs. Howell to come in. Trina suddenly did not feel nearly as brave as she had thought she would. The man's face was wrapped in gauze with only a hole for his eye's and mouth. Trina edged nearer and felt glad to have her friend for moral support.

"Dave, this is Trina Bradley." Doctor Morgan said.

"I am glad to meet you, Mr. Smith," Trina extended her hand. Dave Smith briefly shook hands with her as Trina continued.

"This is my friend Mrs. Howell. We are glad that you are getting along well."

"Why did you want me to meet these people, Doctor?" Dave asked as he shook hands with Mrs. Howell. His voice held a questioning tone. Passive, yet not harsh, as though he wondered why anyone would want to see him.

"I asked the doctor to let us talk to you, Mr. Smith," Trina remembering her mission forgot her nervousness." You see, my parents were the one's you had the accident with. We have been asking about you since. They wouldn't let us see Mama until today. Doctor Morgan is letting her come home. Isn't that great?"

"Yes, Trina. That is great," Dave said. He seemed to show a spark of interest. "I am sorry, but I don't remember the accident nor anything of my past. I only remember what has taken place since I have been here at the hospital. Believe me, I am sorry the accident happened. I don't know if it was my fault or not, but I am sincerely sorry, little Lady." His voice broke and he looked pitiful as he reached with a tissue to wipe his eyes through the hole in the bandage.

Trina's heart filled with sympathy for him.

"No one is to blame. It was an accident, Mr. Smith. That is why I wanted to see you. To tell you that our family understands. You must try hard to get well. Please, may I visit you again?" Trina asked.

Mr. Smith raised his head and looked at Trina through the holes, his question thoughtful and probing, "You said your Mother is going home, Trina. What about your Father?" A feeling of grief and loss swept over Trina. Quickly, she recovered and answered.

"Daddy died in the accident, Mr. Smith. He is with God now. We miss him very much, but it was not your fault and we do not blame you. Please, think about getting well and don't worry. Okay?"

"Thank you," said Mr. Smith, his voice choked with emotion.

"I think we should be going now," Mrs. Howell suggested.

"Do you have any brother's or sister's?" Mr. Smith asked.

"Yes," Trina answered eagerly. "Two Brothers. Joel and Danny. They are to young to visit at the hospital, except we got special permission for them to visit Mama today. When you get out of the hospital you must visit at our home. Would you? Please."

"don't think so, but thank you for the invitation. And thank you both for coming to see me. Goodbye now," he said

"Please, may I visit you again?" Trina begged.

"Well, Trina. Since we are going to be friends let's drop the phony name. Would you call me Dave?" Then he chuckled. "Come to think of it, Dave is a phony name too."

"It's a very nice name, Dave. I will come as often as I can." Trina said. Then she walked across the room and as she went out the door, she called, "Goodbye, Dave."

In the corridor the doctor paused, looking pleased he said, "Trina, I think you are just what the doctor ordered."

"I hope so, Doctor," Trina answered. Then she and Mrs. Howell hurried down the hallway to share their news with the family.

CHAPTER THREE

Everyone had high hopes about Mama's homecoming, on the beautiful spring day in June when the ambulance arrived. They ran to meet them and excitedly kissed Mama hello. The attendants carried her into the house and into the bedroom where Trina led them. Then they sat the wheelchair on the porch and left.

Trina and Joel exchanged glances, wondering what to do to make Mama feel glad that she was home. She lay, quietly looking around the room.

Danny climbed upon the bed and broke the tension by saying,

"I made something for you, Mama."

He unrolled a paper he held in his hand. He had written in bright letters. Welcome home, Mama. I love you.

Tears filled Mama's eyes. She reached a weak hand to brush Danny's hair back.

"I love you, too, Danny," she said. "Everything will be the same when Daddy gets home from his trip. You have all been such good children. Daddy and I will do something real special to show our appreciation."

"Mama," Trina began, but stopped when Mrs. Howell shook her head.

"I am tired. I want to rest now," Mama said.

"Alright, Mama. You rest for awhile." Trina kissed her cheek and they all left the room. Trina closed the door, then gathered Joel and Danny close to her side.

"Please be patient, Boys," she said maturely. "Mama will be better soon. For now, let's enjoy having her home."

Quickly, the boys found something to entertain themselves outside. Trina sat on the sofa beside Mrs. Howell.

"I know you are disappointed, Trina," she said. "We will try to help your Mama remember and pray that she will improve soon."

"She must get well, Mrs. Howell. Joel and Danny need her so much." Trina's lip quivered with disappointment. Mrs. Howell took her in her arms and said,

"You need her to, Dear. I understand how you feel. It's alright." These were the only tears Trina shed in anyone's presence. Quietly, she accepted the role placed upon her and shouldered the added responsibility.

Day and night she cared for Mama. With patience and love they tried to bring her back to reality, but nothing seemed to help as she remained in her illusory world. She ate practically nothing and made no attempt to get out of bed.

To make matters worse, Mrs. Howell came down with an acute attack of arthritis and could hardly manage to care for herself. Trina tried to hurry before her and do the work before she got to it. Finally, in aspiration she said,

"Trina, I hate to admit it but I am becoming another one for you to have to look after, and I won't stand still for that. I am sorry, Dear, but I think we will have to call the welfare for help. We have tried. But Honey, we just can't do it any longer."

"Please, Mrs. Howell. Let the boy's help you home. Let us take care of Mama and the house. We can do it. I know we can."

"Oh Trina. We can hardly get by with all of us helping." Mrs. Howell began to cry.' "I am so sorry to come down like this. I wish I could say that I will be over it in a day or two, but the truth is that when I get an attack like this it usually lasts for months. I don't know what to do."

"Please don't call the welfare Mrs. Howell. They will separate us and put us in different homes. You said so yourself. I can't let the family be broken up. We would all die. They would put Mama in a hospital and she would never get well. Please, I beg you. Let us try for awhile." Trina sobbed until her body shook.

Mrs. Howell gathered her into her arms. "I don't know if it's the right thing or not, but the Lord knows I don't have the heart to cross you, Trina. You promise to come and talk things over with me when you need help. We will see if you can make it. Knowing you, miss grown up young Lady, I would be surprised if you didn't."

One morning Trina dressed in her favorite green plaid. She left her brother's to care for Mama and set out to the hospital to visit Dave. On the way she enjoyed watching the birds and squirrels as they flitted and scampered around. The hospital grounds were beautifully landscaped with trees and flowers and many different kinds of shrubbery.

Trina entered the hospital and no one paid any attention to her as she went through the double doors and walked down the corridor to Dave's room. She hesitated a moment at the door, wondering if he would want to see her again. Oh well, it doesn't matter, she thought. I want to see him.

She gently knocked on the door. No one answered, so she knocked again.

"Come in," a voice said gruffly.

Trina slowly opened the door and hesitated in the doorway. At first, she saw no one. The bed and the chair beside it were empty. Then she saw Dave standing by the window. She stood speechless, taken completely by surprise. It had not occurred to her that he could walk.

"Well, come in. Trina, is it?" His voice lacked a welcome for visitor's.

Trina walked slowly toward him. His face still a little frightening. Trina gathered her courage and said,

"I wanted to visit you and see how you are getting alone, Mr. Smith."

"Oh, you didn't forget me huh," he replied. "Well chalk one up for you. The rest of the world seems to have easily forgotten all about me." Trina ignored the haranguing tone, and said, "You shouldn't feel that way. The people you used to know are most likely very worried about you. They have no way of knowing you are here. I'll bet they are waiting and hoping you will come home. Don't you remember anything yet, Mr. Smith?"

"No, Trina I don't. I am sorry I growled at you," His voice softened as he walked toward her. "What's with this Mr. Smith, anyway? I thought we settled that the other day. Didn't we?"

"Yes, Dave." Trina relaxed and smiled. "I am glad you are able to be up. I didn't know you could walk."

"Yes, I am almost well except for my face. The doctor's say it will be awhile before the bandages come off. I am getting impatient. I want to get out of here." He motioned to the chair and said," Sit down, Trina."

When Trina sat down, she realized how tired she felt. A pain in her stomach reminded, her that in her haste, she had forgotten to eat.

Dave sat on the side of the bed. He wore hospital pajamas that were too large for him. Trina felt a wave of pity for him, and he no longer seemed frightening.

"Do you go anywhere besides this room?" She asked.

"Sure. We have a remarkable solarium. I spend a lot of time there in the sun. There are gardens to walk in, and behind the hospital there is a small lake with swans."

"There really are swans?" Trina's eye's lit up.

"Yes. Would you like to see them?" Dave offered. "We can take a walk together."

Trina hesitated. She wanted to take a walk with Dave, but she realized that she could not for she must go home to see about Mama and the boys.

"I would like that very much," she said. "But I don't have time today. I have to go to the grocery store and then home. I promised Joel that 1 wouldn't be gone long."

"Maybe you can come again then," Dave suggested.

"Oh, yes. I will," Trina accepted gladly.

"Come anytime you can, Trina," Dave said. "I will be here."

"Maybe I can come the day after tomorrow, Dave," Trina said.

Dave rose as Trina stood to go. He placed a hand tenderly on her shoulder. "You have a lot of responsibility for a little girl, don't you? Do you have grandparents or someone who can give you a hand?"

"No, Now that Daddy is gone it's just Mama and us kids alone. Of course, Mrs. Howell did help us but she had an attack of arthritis and had to go home."

"Doesn't anyone from the church or Red Cross, or something like that come around to offer help?" He queried,

"No, Sir. We keep quiet because we are afraid the welfare people will separate us. We make it fine except . . ." she paused.

"Except what, Trina?" Dave asked sympathetically.

"Except school starts in a few weeks and we have all outgrown our clothes," Trina confided. "I must come up with a way to get us some new ones before school begins. If we don't go, the truant officer will find out that Mama is sick, and us kids are taking care of her. Then they would probably take Mama to a hospital, where she never will get well, and they will separate the boys and me, and we will never see each other again," Trina began to cry.

"Hey. Whoa there. Partner. Don't cry," Dave comforted. "Maybe I can think of a way to help."

Trina walked home happier than she had been in a long time. She did not really expect Dave to help them, because how could he? He had no job and no idea of when he would be released from the hospital. Yet she felt the load she carried to be considerably lighter. How wonderful to have someone to confide in. Trina knew that Dave would never betray her trust.

Trina sat her groceries down and went immediately to tend Mama. Joel, as usual had fulfilled her expectations. He sat reading a book as Mama tried to pay attention. She smiled weakly when she saw Trina.

"'bout time you got back," Joel growled, "We are starved."

"I'm sorry, Joel. We will cook dinner right away, Danny and I are going to bake a chocolate cake. Right Danny?" Trina's good nature spread to the boy's. The house quickly came alive with activity as they tackled the chores together.

Soon dinner awaited. The aroma of fresh baked cake filled the air. Trina helped Mama freshen up, then made a decision.

"Mama, I want you to sit in your chair and have dinner with us tonight. It will be wonderful for us to eat together like we used to."

"But it won't be like it used to be, Trina. Your Daddy hasn't come home from his trip yet," Lorraine said pitifully,

"Of course it will be better when Daddy gets home, Mama," Trina decided to humor her. "But until then, I think it would be nice if you have dinner with Danny, Joel, and Me. Okay?"

Trina did not wait for an answer. She said,

"Danny, bring Mama's chair. We are going to get her up for dinner."

"Hooray," yelled Danny, and ran excitedly to bring the chair.

Working together, Trina and Joel lifted Mama into the chair. Happily, Joel rolled her to the kitchen. They enjoyed their dinner more than any night since the accident.

Trina visited Dave every time she could squeeze in a visit with her shopping schedule. They became friends as they shared the precious time they had together,

Trina's favorite time was spent at the lake watching the swans. They were beautiful as they promenaded over the blue water. It was on such a day that Trina realized how much Dave had come to mean to her. He would soon be leaving the hospital for his facial burns improved every day. She felt happy that he would soon be well, but she knew that when he left the hospital she may not see him again.

"Where will you go, Dave?" She asked passively,

"Well, Trina," Dave shared. "I may not go anywhere for a while. I have been offered a job here at the hospital. The gardener took a leave of absence due to illness. Doctor Morgan thought I might be interested so he offered me the job."

Tears glistened in Trina's eye's as she looked affectionately at her friend. "Oh, Dave. I am so glad. That means we can still be friends. You can come over to my house and meet Mama and the boys. Will you?"

"I don't see why not, Trina," Dave said fondly, "I think I would like that very much, and Trina, even if we should be parted sometime we will always "be friends. Agreed?" Dave reached and tenderly placed a hand on Trina's cheek. Gently with his other hand he wiped away a tear that escaped her eye and ran down her pretty face,

"Agreed?" He repeated, and his smile filled Trina's heart with happiness.

"Agreed." She smiled back at Dave.

"So then why do you still have that worried look on your face, little Lady?" Dave released her and sat back to listen.

"I didn't want to bother you with our problems, Dave, but I have no one else that I can trust. Except Mrs. Howell of course. School starts next week and we have no money for clothes and book rent." She tried bravely to keep from crying again.

"I haven't forgotten, Trina. That is why I am anxious to take the gardener's job. We will be able to shop for clothing for you and the boy's," Dave volunteered.

"But Dave," Trina objected. "We are not your responsibility. You will need what you make to pay your own bills."

"No. It won't take much for me. I want to help, Trina, Please. After all, we are partners aren't we?"

"Of course we are, Dave," Trina nodded.

"I have an idea. I will talk to the hospital administrator, maybe we can work something out about an advance on my salary. If so, We can shop tomorrow. You come in the morning, and I should know something by then."

Dave's depression had disappeared since he and Trina were spending time together, for his heart was filled with affection for his young friend.

By some miracle Dave talked himself into receiving a paycheck before working a day on his new job. Trina brought the boy's with her so they could fit them. They enjoyed a wonderful day, and Danny and Joel immediately fell in love with Dave.

"Come home with us Dave," Danny begged when the shopping was completed,

"Not this time, Danny," Dave said, "I would like to but I don't want to alarm your Mother, The bandages might make her nervous, I will come soon. That is a promise,"

The children talked excitedly on the way home,

"You were right Trina," Joel declared, "Dave is terrific."

"Mama, we got new school clothes," Danny said, when they arrived at home. He held up a blue shirt, "Look, this is my favorite,"

Mama tried to smile, but it was lost in the effort,

"That is nice, Danny," she whispered weakly, "Daddy will like it. He likes blue." Her interest faded. Trina gathered up the treasured possessions and motioned for the others to follow as she left the room.

As they prepared dinner Danny asked," Where do you suppose Dave will go when he leaves the hospital, Trina?"

"I am hoping he will stay around here," Trina answered.

"Let's tell him how much we want him to stay," Danny suggested.

"I will tell him tomorrow," Trina promised.

After dinner Trina put a load of clothes in the washing machine, then joined her brother's in the living room.

"I sure am glad Dad bought the washer and dryer," she said, "Without them I would be sunk."

Danny sat, engrossed in a mystery movie on TV, Trina sat on the sofa beside Joel,

"Trina do you think Mama will ever get well?" Joel asked sadly,

"I don't know, Joel, We just have to take care of her and keep hoping," Trina said. "We must have faith."

"I know," Joel muttered, then turned his attention to the movie.

The next thing Trina knew Danny was shaking her and saying, "Wake up Trina. The movie is over. Boy, I knew it was the guy from the service station all along. Didn't I say so, Joel."

"Yes, Danny, You did," Joel agreed. "Go on, let's go to bed,"

"You go ahead, I want to look in on Mama," Trina said.

She opened the door and peeked in, Mama slept peacefully and despite her failing illness she looked beautiful with her long dark hair spread over the pillow,

A lump came in Trina's throat, "Oh, Mama. You must get well. We need you," she whispered, Tears glistened in her eyes as she turned to go up the stairs.

She opened the door to the boys' room. They were in bed. Trina sat on the foot of Danny's bed and solemnly said,

"Joel and Danny, do you remember how Mama always taught us to pray and believe that God will answer our prayers?"

Both boys nodded. They were awed by their sister's mood,

"Well," Trina went on. "I believe that if we pray real hard, and believe strong enough that God will help Mama get well. Do you believe it too?"

"If you say so, Trina," Joel said.

"I believe, Trina," Danny said assuringly,

"Then we will pray every night until Mama is well," Trina said,

"Let's pray for Dave to stay here and be our friend," Danny suggested.

"Wait. I will be right back," Trina said as she ran out of the room. In a few minutes she returned with the family Bible, she opened it and read;

"The Lord is my Shepard, I shall not want. He maketh me to lie down in green pastures. He leadeth me beside the still waters. He restoreth my soul. He leadeth me in the paths of righteousness for his namesake.

Yea, though I walk through the valley of the shadow of death, I will fear no evil; for thou art with me: Thy rod and thy staff they comfort me, Thou preparest a table before me in the presence of mine enemies; Thou anointest my head with oil, my cup runneth over. Surely goodness and mercy shall follow me all the days of my life, and I will dwell in the house of the Lord forever."

She closed the book and silently the three slipped off the bed to their knees.

They cried earnest tears as they poured their heart out to the God whom their parents had taught them to love. When they finished, Trina tucked her brother's in and kissed them goodnight. Then she went to bed and slept soundly believing that God had heard and would surely answer their prayers.

She arose early the next morning, dressed hurriedly and went outside. She climbed the observation tree to her favorite limb. As she looked out over the neighborhood, she held on to her exuberance from the night before. Hope filled her being and she felt good.

"Thank you, God," she said. "And if you please, let Dave stay in Westville so that we can have him for our very own."

I loved Daddy very much, she thought. But now that he is gone to be with God I need someone like Dave. He understands and cares about us.

With that thought she climbed down the tree and hurried to cook breakfast and do her chores. She felt so excited she could hardly wait to get to the hospital.

She hurried down the corridor and knocked on Dave's door. No one answered. She opened the door enough to peek in. The tidy room looked as though no one occupied it, and the bed stood neatly made, but where was Dave?

CHAPTER FOUR

Trina's heart sank as she surveyed the room. Obviously Dave had been moved. But Where and why? Fear gripped her at the thought of Dave being lost to her and the family. Then she seemed to hear Dave's voice say,

"Trina, no matter if we are apart, we will always be friends. Nothing can change that."

With effort she bolstered her courage and decided to ask about Dave at the nurses station. Nurses in crisp, white uniforms dashed to and fro but she recognized none. Timidly she approached the desk.

"Hello. May I help you?" The nurse behind the desk asked.

"Yes Ma'am," Trina said shyly. "I came to visit Dave Smith, but he is not in his room. I wondered if you can tell me where he is."

"Let me check for you," she said. She turned to a rack containing medical records and began shuffling through them. When she had looked at all of them she turned.

"I am sorry, Dear. But I don't find a Dave Smith here."

"But he must be here," Trina insisted. "I saw him yesterday."

"Then he must have been released. I assure you that he is not a patient on this wing or I would have his record right here." Trina could not believe this was happening. She stood motionless, tears brimming her eyes.

"But someone must know where he is," Trina insisted. "Surely the nurses that were on duty know where to find him."

"I am sorry, but the nurses work on a rotating basis. This is our first shift on this floor." She gave Trina a slight smile, then said, "Excuse me, I must get to my work."

Trina felt crushed. She could not believe that Dave would go away without telling her. Her heart heavy, she started for home. Joel and Danny met her anxiously awaiting news from Dave. Trina dreaded telling them that Dave was gone.

"Boy's, Dave is . . ." she began to cry. Angrily she wiped her eye's with her fist. She did not like to appear weak before the boy's. Now here she stood, coming unglued before their eye's.

"What's wrong, Trina," Joel asked.

Trina related the peculiar news. The boy's stood shocked and unbelieving.

"What are we going to do, Trina?" Danny asked, in despair.

"I don't know of anything we can do," answered Trina. "We will have to wait until Dave gets in touch with us."

"I'm scared. What if we never hear from him again," voiced Danny.

"Then we will take care of Mama and each other," Trina regained her composure. "That is what Daddy and Dave would expect of us."

The next morning Trina was busily doing the chores when Danny ran up the lane yelling,

"Trina, we got a letter. Hurry."

Trina ran to meet him as Joel ran around the house to join them. Hastily Trina tore open the envelope. She took out a single sheet of yellow paper, and went weak with relief,

"It's from Dave." She said.

"Hurry and read it," her brother's said in unison.

Trina read; Dear Trina, Joel and Danny, I am sorry to leave without saying goodbye, but I must. The doctors have decided the burns on my face are not healing as well as they thought. They are sending me to Saint Louis to a burn trauma center to have plastic surgery. Believe me, if it were not necessary I would not go away and leave you. Please, I want all of you to be brave and strong. Take care of your Mama and yourselves. Study hard to keep up your grades in school. I will be thinking of you constantly, and as soon as they release me I will return. I love you all. Remember *me* in your prayers and rest assured mine will be for you, Love, Dave.

"I knew Dave wouldn't leave unless he had a good reason," Trina said. Her heart seemed to sprout wings.

Shortly before school vacation they received still another letter from Dave. All is going well, he wrote. I am looking forward to seeing you all for Christmas if I am released in time.

This thrilled the children and they began making their plans for Christmas.

"Hey Trina." Danny's voice aroused Trina from her reverie. "How long have I been daydreaming?" She whispered. She had lost all track of the present as she relived the past.

She arose and went downstairs.

"Trina, there is no school tomorrow. May we go downtown and see the Christmas decorations?" Danny asked excitedly.

"Yes." Trina agreed. "I love to hear the chimes play carols." "Trina, where do you suppose we can find a tree?" Joel asked, "I don't know. But we will think of something," she said, "Let's go up to the attic and look for the decorations" Daddy had put the box of decorations up, so they did not know exactly where to find them,

"Jeez, it's cold up here," Danny said, "let's hurry." Trina moved some old clothing and found a trunk underneath. "I wonder what is in here. There should be a key somewhere." The boy's quickly forgot their mission and joined her. Trina found the key in a dresser drawer and opened the trunk. All they could see was white tissue paper. Trina lifted it and gave a cry of surprise,

"Oooah, it's Mama's wedding gown," She held it up to her chin.

The long skirt and train rippled to the floor,

"Mama must have looked like a Princess at her wedding," Trina said "Hey, look," Joel reached into the trunk and picked something up.

He brought it out and opened his hand,

"It is a brooch," Trina asserted. "My, isn't it beautiful?" Trina took the brooch and examined it. Even to her untrained eye it was a treasure. In the center stood a Cameo, Surrounding it were diamonds and rubies, alternating in a circle, inset with pearl and mounted in gold. Its beauty was breathtaking.

"Maybe we can sell it and get some money for Christmas," Danny suggested,

"Oh Danny." Trina said, "We couldn't do that. This is precious to Mama. It belongs to her."

"But Trina. Mama don't even remember it and we need the money-real bad. You know we do. We need clothes and we don't have boots to wear in the snow." Danny pleaded.

"Danny is right, Trina," Joel said solemnly. "Its not doing Mama any good and we need the money."

Trina held the treasure in her hand admiring its detail. At last she agreed. "I know we need the money. I suppose we can take it with us into the city tomorrow and see what it is worth."

"Alright," Joel said. "Now lets find the decorations."

They were not hard to find once they set their minds to looking and soon they were on their way downstairs with Trina clutching the brooch tightly in her hand.

The next morning they set out for the city. The chimes permeated the air. Trina filled with exuberance, sang along;

"0, come all ye faithful, joyful and triumphant, come ye, o come ye, to Bethlehem."

The streets were crowded with shoppers who smiled and shouted holiday greetings to each other. At Masons, Danny peered in the window at a Snow White and the seven Dwarfs, in animated figures. Dopey waddled to the window and tipped his hat to them, as they laughed.

The next window held an elaborate electric train winding around a track and through tunnels.

"Boy," Danny wished. "I hope I get that for Christmas."

They walked on until they came to a window where Santa sat talking to children. He held each on his knee as their turn came.

Observing the bag of goodies Santa handed each child in the line, Trina and her brother's quickly entered into a conspiracy to obtain one for themselves. They joined the line and exited the store with peals of laughter with their coveted sack in hand after the humbling experience of sitting on Santa's lap.

Then to return to the business at hand they entered Jacobsons House of Jewelry. A nice looking man in a grey suit stood behind the counter waiting on a lady. When she left, he jovially addressed the children.

"Good morning. May I help you," his smile helped them muster the courage to show him the brooch.

"We want to know how much money we can get for this," Trina said.

"Well now, What do we have here?" He took the brooch and picked up a gadget, placed it to his eye and looked at the brooch turning it this way and that. At last, he said,

"Where did you children get such a brooch."

"It belongs to our Mother," Trina explained. "She is not well, and is not able to come downtown. We need the money. What do you think the brooch is worth?"

"This brooch is valuable," he said. "I would say it is worth one thousand dollars."

"Wow," Joel exclaimed, while Trina's eyes widened in surprise.

"You children are telling me the truth about where you got this now aren't you?" The jeweler asked.

"It belongs to my Mama," Danny spoke for the first time since entering the store.

"Alright, I believe you, but I cannot possibly buy this fine piece of jewelry without your mothers written permission. Since she is ill, I will consider buying it if you bring written permission with her signature," he handed the brooch to Trina, "May I give you some Advice?"

Trina nodded.

"Be careful of where you let this brooch be seen," he warned. "Some dealers are not above trying to do you out of it. Our store has built our reputation on honesty and fair dealings. Come back to me if you have your mother's written permission. Okay?"

"Yes, Sir." Trina left the store with Joel and Danny close behind.

"Trina," Joel asked. "Are you going to ask Mama to sign a paper?" "I am not sure she can, Joel," Trina answered. "We will see." As they turned to start their journey home, Trina's eye caught sight of a sign in a window across the street. It read; Premium Prices for Virgin Hair.

Trina knew the store sold wigs for the window held several manikins modeling them. She suddenly realized that she possessed at least one thing she could sell to have money for a nice Christmas. She caught the glimmer of an idea, but she must get away from the boy's for awhile.

"Joel, I want to look at some dresses at the Junior Miss shop, you and Danny watch the trains in Masons window for a little while," she urged.

"But Trina, why do you want to look at dresses. You don't have any money to buy one." Joel objected.

"I know," Trina insisted. I just want to look. Please, Joel."

Danny accepted the opportunity enthusiastically, and Joel reluctantly agreed.

Trina crossed the street and stopped in front of the wig shop. She felt a lump in her throat as she raised her hand to run it over her soft, silky hair cascading over her shoulders in dark natural curls.

She gathered her courage and went inside. The store seemed to be owned by Orientals. Behind the counter stood a short man, and toward the back of the store two oriental ladies stood at dressing tables working on wigs.

The proprietor smiled at Trina and gave a funny bow.

"May I be of service to you, Miss?" He asked.

"Yes, Sir," Trina said timidly. "I saw the sign in the window."

"Oh," the man's interest peaked. "Do you want to sell your hair, Young Lady?"

The way he looked at Trina made her nervous. She felt an urge to run out the door.

"How much will you pay for my hair?" She asked softly.

He came from behind the counter and walked around Trina looking at her hair. He reached a hand to feel it and Trina winced as she felt his fingers go through her hair and touch her scalp.

"It is certainly virgin hair," he said, "No tints or bleach on this head. Very nice."

It seemed forever before he said, "I'll pay you fifty dollars."

The greedy look in his eye's gave Trina the creeps.
She figured he must be dishonest to offer money
for her hair without insisting on her parents
permission, but at her age if she did any dealing
at all it would have to be with this sort. The
honest man at the jewelry store had convinced
her of that.

"I want to think it over," Trina decided. "If I
decide to do it, I will come back tomorrow."

"Very well," he seemed irritated by her hesitancy.
"But be here before noon, mind you."

Trina dashed out the door and joined her brother's
for the walk home, her mind working furiously
all the way.

When they tried to talk to Mama about the
brooch that night they were surprised when she
held it to her and smiled.

"Your Daddy gave this to me," she said, her eyes
shining. "He brought it to me when he came
home from the service. You ask Daddy if you can
sell it, Trina."

"But Mama," Trina tried to explain. "Daddy is
not here and we need the money. It is only a

week until Christmas, and the boys need boots, Mama."

Trina knew she was not getting through to Mama when the glazed look returned to her eyes. She sighed with disappointment as Mama said, "You ask Daddy, Trina. Daddy will be home soon. You will see."

"It's no use," Joel said sadly. "Mama is never going to get well, Trina. Nothing is ever going to get better. Don't you see. We can't live like this forever."

He rushed out of the room before anyone could see him cry. He ran up the stairs with Danny on his heels. Trina quickly made her decision. Her heart beat fast as she entered the store the next morning. No one was in sight. Once more she ran her hand down her velvet like hair. It looked much like Mama's. Trina treasured it more because of this.

"Well, I see you made up your mind." The voice startled her. She turned to see the man whom she talked to the day before. She felt afraid and wished it was over and she could go. She mustered every bit of courage she could and said,

"Yes, Sir. I will sell you my hair."

"Very well then." He circled Trina and she shrank inside as once more he fondled her hair.

"Come with me." He abruptly started toward the back of the store. Suddenly, Trina felt terrified as she wondered what this strange man might do to her if they were in that back room alone. Then she remembered how much her brother's needed boots. She followed him through the door.

To Trina's surprise, when she entered she saw one of the young lady's she remembered from yesterday standing at a dressing table working on wigs. Trina swallowed hard and said a silent thanks. The man spoke,

"Lileen, please cut this young lady's hair. She has bravely decided to sell it to us,"

The lady gave a small bow and motioned for Trina to sit in a chair. She smiled slightly at Trina through the large mirror. Trina looked at herself in the mirror, and her reflection seemed to say accusingly, "Trina Bradley, what are you doing here?"

The lady fastened a cape around Trina's neck, then reached for her scissors. Trina thought she would have a heart attack as she held up the top of her hair and whack; whack, it gave way to the scissors.

Swiftly, she raised the left side. Whack; whack, again long strands of silken beauty fell at the bidding of those businesslike scissors.

Trina glanced down at her tresses lying on the shiny floor that looked as though it were constantly polished. She felt even the floor joined the conspiracy to separate her from her esteemed treasure.

"We are finished now." The lady removed the cape and dismissed Trina with a bow, Trina looked into the mirror and was astonished to see Joel's face looking back at her. Her hair now pixie short, she looked so much like her brother she stared transfixed,

"You may go now. Here is your money," The man reappeared and handed her some bills. Trina took the money and timidly counted two twenties and a ten. She felt relived that the man did not try to cheat her after all. She realized that it had only been her imagination,

"Thank you," she said and quickly took her leave.

Trina decided to go to Bradburies thrift store and see if she could find boots for the boy's and possibly some other gifts. After she bought gifts for the family and Dave she saw a bright Christmassy scarf and counted enough remaining money to pay for it for herself. Outside, she put down her bulky packages and looking at her reflection in the store window, tied the scarf around her head.

"There," she said. "No one will know that my hair is gone as long as I wear the scarf."

She trudged toward home carrying her parcels and feeling very satisfied and happy. Now if Dave came their Christmas would be perfect.

Joel and Danny awaited her with a surprise of their own. They ushered her into the living room and showed her a beautifully decorated tree.

"It's beautiful," she exclaimed. "But where did you get it?"

"I walked over to Maple street where a man was selling them from a truck," Joel explained excitedly. "I helped him for awhile, and he gave me one."

Happily, they placed the parcels Trina brought around the tree, and proudly admired their handiwork as they stood with bright smiles, congratulating *one* another.

On Christmas eve Danny and Joel went to visit Mrs. Howell. Trina worked happily around the kitchen preparing for her Christmas dinner. She took her time about answering a knock on the door, for she thought it was the boy's teasing. When she swiftly pulled the door back she looked right into the chest of a man. She stopped short and allowed her gaze to move up the slender frame.

When the scream left her lips it sounded so foreign that she thought it came from someone else.

"Hi Trina. I didn't mean to startle you. Didn't you get my letters I wrote to you from the hospital in Saint Louis?"

Trina paled and felt she was going to faint. She struggled to speak, but no sound came.

"I am sorry. I had no idea I looked so frightening," he said. "Of course, this is the first time you have seen my face."

Trina stood frozen. Never had she been so shocked and surprised.

"Doggoneit, Girl. Will you say something. It's me, Dave." "Your not Dave," Trina finally regained the ability to speak. "You're my Daddy."

The blow nearly knocked Dave off his feet. His forehead wrinkled in distress.

"What are you talking about, Trina? Has all this responsibility affected your thinking facility?"

"No. I know what I am saying. I tell you, you are my Daddy. I don't know how it happened. They must have gotten you mixed up with the other man in the accident. Please, believe me. You are not Dave at all. You are Dan Bradley. Mama keeps saying over and over that you are coming home. How could she have known?"

"Trina, I find this hard to believe. I don't know what to say."

"Come in, I will show you." Trina moved aside and he entered the living room, Trina took a picture album from a shelf and turned the pages until she found what she wanted.

"Look here. This is my Parents." She held it where he could look at the photograph. He swayed, and quickly sat down on the sofa.

"I can't believe it. This just cannot be," he shook his head in amazement.

"We must do something to prepare Joel and Danny," Trina said. "They will be home any minute now."

He sat in stunned silence.

"Do you believe me now?" Trina pleaded.

"I don't know what to say," tears filled his eyes.

Trina placed an arm over his shoulder. "Don't cry, Daddy," she comforted. "I am so happy to see you. I love you, Daddy."

Suddenly he reached and took her in his arms. Together their tears mingled as they held each other and wept. At last Trina pushed back and looked at his face.

"Do you remember anything at all, Daddy?" She asked. "No, Trina. I remember nothing that happened before the accident," "Well, never you mind," Trina said assuredly. "You are at home again and we can take care of each other. After awhile you will remember. I know you will, Daddy,"

In their enchantment of finding each other, they forgot about the boy's. Suddenly the door burst open and Danny and Joel entered happily talking away to each other. When they saw their visitor, they stopped and stared. Both faces turned to ashes as they saw the unbelievable.

"Boys, let me explain," Trina started toward them.

"Daddy," Danny yelled. He ran across the room and jumped, landing in his Daddy's arms. "I thought you were dead," he sobbed,

"I know. Son. I know," he held him close. Then put him down and turned to Joel. As he reached to embrace him, Joel ran into his arms crying.

"We have to talk about this, Joel," he said. "Let's sit down." Everyone sat as near their Dad as possible. Joel said,

"Daddy, I don't understand. Dave is supposed to come today. We thought you were dead."

"Let me explain, Son. First let's get this settled. There is no Dave Smith. Trina has convinced me that the authorities made a mistake when the accident happened. Since I cannot remember, I did not know that you were my family. From now on I will go back to being Dan Bradley. But we have a problem. This could have an unsuitable affect on your mother. We must be careful. It could cause her a lot of harm if we don't handle it right. We won't tell her that I am here until we decide the best way to go about it. Agreed?"

"Yes," the children agreed.

"Oh, I am so glad to know the three of you are my children," Daddy said. "I fell in love with you all so completely. I love you." Again they were lost in a barrage of hugs and kisses.

"Trina," Mama's voice carried into the room and brought them back to their present problem.

CHAPTER FIVE

While Trina attended Mama, the boy's took Daddy and went up to their room. When Trina joined them Daddy said "Say, Trina, I want to get up in the morning and climb the observation tree. Would you like to join me?"

"Daddy, you remember our tree," Trina said excitedly,

"Not exactly, Honey," Daddy explained. "Joel and Danny told me about it. It sounds great though,"

"Oh, Daddy, I would love to climb the tree with you," Trina said. She lay awake for a long time after she went to bed, thinking about the events of the day,

Trina awakened at dawn and hurriedly dressed, taking time to secure her scarf over her short hair.

Then she was off to keep her rendezvous with Daddy, It was still to dark to see very far up the tree, but she was so familiar with each limb she could almost have climbed it with her eyes shut.

When she almost reached the top she heard a voice say,

"I thought you had forgotten, Sleepyhead."

"Oh, Daddy. I wouldn't forget," she replied.

Daddy laughed. That wonderful, lovely sounding laugh. Trina thought nothing had ever sounded so good, as she took her place beside him.

"Aaah, this place is terrific." He planted a kiss on her cheek, "Good morning, Princess. I love you."

"I love you too, Daddy," Trina said. "It's wonderful to be here in our tree together again."

Trina pointed to various houses over the neighborhood as it grew lighter, but Daddy did not remember.

"I have confidence that my memory will return now that I am at home with my family," Daddy said.

"Daddy, we must tell Mama that you are home right away. She has said all along that you were coming home. She did not accept for a minute that you were dead, even after we told her about the funeral."

"That's right," Daddy said. "They would have held a funeral. Where was it, Trina?"

"At the funeral home on Jackson street. Mrs. Howell found a minister who conducted the service," Trina smiled. "He had cold hands and sweaty palms."

"Really?" queried Daddy.

"Yes," Trina said. "Daddy, I never felt satisfied about that funeral. Somehow it seemed there was something missing."

Daddy laughed. "I guess it was me."

Trina joined him in laughter and the release felt good. Finally, Daddy grew solemn and said, "I know the truck driver died in the accident, Trina. I hope we can locate his family and tell them how sorry we feel about it."

"Yes," agreed Trina. "I hope we can.

"It's getting cold, Sweetheart," Daddy said. "Maybe we should go in." They climbed down the tree.

In the kitchen they set about cooking breakfast. Soon Joel and Danny came running excitedly down the stairs.

"Good morning, Daddy," they embraced him lovingly,

"Lets have breakfast before we open our gifts," Trina suggested. "By then, Mama will be awake and maybe she will feel like joining us."

They talked and laughed as they ate, enjoyed the meal. In their happiness they forgot to keep their voices down.

Suddenly a shadow fell across the table. They all looked up, startled as the unexpected miracle moved toward them,

"Dan," Mama said. She swayed and caught the door facing. Instantly Daddy moved across the room and took her in his arms. As they held each other, Trina sat immobilized, eyes wide with the shock of Mama standing. Both boys sat frozen with surprise,

"Dan, I am so glad you are home," Mama said at last, "I have been ill and the children have taken care of me, I told them you would be proud of them,"

"Yes Darling," Daddy released Mama and gently led her to a chair, "I am proud of you all.

Mama trembled from weakness, but she smiled and her face glowed.

"Trina, want to get Mama some coffee?" Daddy's question seemed to release Trina so she could move again. She ran around the table to embrace them both,

"Mama you believed all along that Daddy would come home. You were right, I love you, Mama. This is the best Christmas ever."

"Yes, it is the best," Daddy held Mama's hand. "Honey, I am sorry I have been away so long. It's going to be different now,"

"Lets open the gifts now," Danny shouted, as he headed for the living room.

The family followed. Soon the gifts were distributed, and the boy's thrilled at their new boots, and started pulling them on. Daddy brought gifts and hid them outside until morning when everyone was still sleeping before bringing them in and placing them under the tree along with Trina's.

"Oh, Boy," Danny yelled when he opened his gift and found an eighteen wheeler truck. Joel found an intricate model airplane in his wrapper. "Thanks Dad," he said, "You sure picked the right gift for me. I am going to be a pilot."

"I am glad, Joel," Daddy said.

Mama opened hers and found a charm bracelet. She smiled at her family as Daddy fastened it around her wrist.

"This is yours, Daddy," Trina handed a small package to him as she added, "I thought I was buying it for Dave."

Everyone enjoyed a good laugh until Mama said, "who is Dave?"

"It's not important, Dear. I will tell you all about it later," Daddy said. Then to Trina he said,

"Thank you, Hon. I needed a wallet. Now you open your gift."

Trina slowly unwrapped her gift. Her heart fluttered nervously as she held up a tortoise shell headband in delicate pink and blue shades. Fear gripped her as she realized the family knew nothing about her hair. She had been careful to wear the scarf, and though they may have wondered about it they had said nothing. But now, the moment of truth had arrived.

"It is pretty," Mama said.

"Put it on, Honey," Daddy urged. "Come to think of it, I haven't seen that pretty hair of yours since I have been home. I remember how lovely it looked in the sunshine as we sat by the lake at the hospital. As soon as I saw this band in the store, I knew it was meant for you."

"Thank you, Daddy," Trina said weakly. "I will put it on later."

She quickly pushed it back into the box. Daddy furrowed his brow.

"Put it on now, Trina. I want to see you wear it," he said.

Trina had never passed up an opportunity to please Daddy. Sudden tears filled her eyes. She dropped her head. She did not know what to do. She knew that sooner or later she would have to tell them about her hair, but now that the time had come she did not know how to go about it.

Daddy purchasing this band because he liked her hair only added to her dread of telling what she had done.

"What's wrong, Trina?" Danny asked.

"Put the pretty band on for Daddy, Trina," Mama begged.

Still Trina sat Silently looking down at the floor. The family became more concerned because this was so unlike Trina.

Daddy reached over and took hold of the scarf. One tug and it slid off her head. Shock spread over his face as he held the scarf in his hand.

Trina, what happened to your hair?" Danny shouted.

Trina sat mortified as everyone stared at her. She tried to think of something to say but her throat felt frozen as though she would never be able to speak again.

"Trina, I want you to tell me right now what happened to your hair," Daddy's voice held the no nonsense tone that Trina remembered so well.

Daddy had always been easygoing and good natured, but when his voice held that tone no one doubted that whatever problem existed would be dealt with seriously.

"Yes, Sir," Trina whispered. She raised her tear streaked face to look at her family. Then her gaze rested on Daddy.

"Well?" Daddy questioned.

"I sold it to buy Christmas gifts," she blurted out, then burst into tears all over again.

"But what happened to the brooch?" Joel asked in awe.

"I just couldn't sell Mamas brooch. It meant so much to her," Trina confessed. "I put it back in the trunk."

"Oh, Trina. You wonderful, precious sweetheart," Daddy sat beside her and took her in his arms. Mama reached out to hold her hand.

"You did that for us?" Joel squeaked.

Danny for once stood quietly, shocked into silence.

"We didn't have any money. Daddy," Trina offered at last. "I promised Joel and Danny that we were going to have a nice Christmas. They have been so good to help without complaining. I just had to make this a happy Christmas for them."

"Now, that's alright, Honey," Daddy said soothingly. "You have a heart full of love, Trina. Such unselfishness calls for a lot of respect. I know that I have the most wonderful Daughter in the world, and you needn't worry about the headband. Why, in no time at all your hair will be grown out again. Anyway, you look cute with short hair. Doesn't she, Boys?"

"You look like Joel," Danny said.

"I know," Trina sniffled. She raised her head to look at her beloved family, once more.

"I am proud of you," Daddy said. "Look, Lorriane, Trina loved the family so much she sold her hair to give us a happy Christmas. Aren't you proud of her?"

"Yes," Mama said weakly, but happily. She squeezed Trina's hand.

"I am very proud of you, Trina," she said.

"So are we, Trina," Joel agreed. "This is the best Christmas!"

"You are the best Sister anyone ever had, Trina," Danny said.

"Thank you all," Trina smiled as Danny remembered his gifts and returned to enjoy them.

"Well, Family," Daddy said, "What do you say we sing some carols before we tackle the holiday dinner?"

Trina wiped away the last of the tears,

"I think that would be wonderful, Daddy, Don't you, Mama?"

"Yes, wonderful," Mama said. Then her lovely soprano voice filled the air as she began to sing;

0', come, all ye faithful joyful and triumphant.

Come ye, o come ye, to Bethlehem,

Trina and Daddy looked at each other and smiled. Pride filled Daddy's voice as he joined in with Mama,

Come and behold Him, born the King of Angels.

0, come, let us adore Him,

0, come, let us adore Him,

0, come, let us adore Him,

Christ the Lord,

Trina joined in. Then Joel and Danny until their voices blended in harmony, lifting their hearts with thanksgiving and worship of the Holy Child, whose birthday they celebrated.

As Trina lovingly swept her gaze from one to the other, her heart filled with hope. She knew that from this day forward things were going to be better for them. Soon Mama would be well, and Daddy would have his memory return.

She could take her place as the young girl she was, Joel and Danny could join the boy scouts and play ball. Trina knew as surely as though it were already true that their lives would return to normal.

She thought of Mrs. Howell and made a mental note to see that she would be repaid for her unselfish help she so lovingly gave.

Trina ran her hand over her short hair. Suddenly, she realized that she did like it, very much.

It's pretty« she thought. And why not? But even if it were not pretty, I would do it over again. After it is for the best family in the whole world. MY FAMILY.